This book belongs to:

isure &

. . . .

Faber has published children's books since 1929. T. S. Eliot's *Old Possum's Book of Practical Cats* and Ted Hughes' *The Iron Man* were amongst the first. Our catalogue at the time said that 'it is by reading such books that children learn the difference between the shoddy and the genuine'. We still believe in the power of reading to transform children's lives. We pride ourselves on responsible editing and think our books deliver on their promise. We hope they grow a love of reading, kindle curiosity and nurture empathy. Our aim is to publish excellent, kind and inclusive books in which all children feel represented and important.

First published in the UK in 2021,
First published in the US in 2021,
by Faber and Faber Limited,
Bloomsbury House,
74–77 Great Russell Street,
London WC1B 3DA.

Printed in the UK.

A CIP record for this book is available from the British Library.

HB ISBN 978–0–571–35830–4
PB ISBN 978–0–571–35831–1

5 7 9 10 8 6

For Lucy
J. C.

For Agnes
K. G.

What Happened to You?

James Catchpole

Illustrated by
Karen George

faber

Joe was playing his favourite game.

It had sharks.

And possibly crocodiles.

But crocodiles and sharks were no match for pirates like Joe.

"Not this time, Señor Sharkface!"

Sharks were easy
compared to kids
Joe hadn't met yet.

"YOU'VE ONLY GOT ONE LEG!"

said a kid.

"Yup," said Joe.
"And you've just
squashed my shark."

"What happened
to you?"
said the kid.

But Joe didn't feel like
telling *that* story,
so he just said,
"What do *you* think?"

"Ummm . . ."

The **kid** didn't know
how to answer that.

But another kid did.

"Did it fall off?"

"No,"
said Joe.

A third kid thought that was silly. "Legs don't fall off," she said.

Kid Number Four agreed. He asked, "Was it a burglar?"

Then Kid Two thought very hard, and said, "Did it fall off . . . in the toilet?"

"No, and . . . no," said Joe.

"This is a trick, isn't it?
You're hiding it," said Kid Five.

"NO!" said Joe.
"And stop staring
at my bottom."

There were more questions . . .   which Joe did try to answer

though some of them . . .

were a bit silly.

"Yes," said Joe.
"It was a thousand lions."

"REALLY?" said the kids.

"**No!**" shouted Joe.

Joe was playing his game again.
But this time, Kid One said . . .

"Is that a crocodile
down there?"

And Joe said,
"Yes, I think so."

"My name is Simone," said Kid One.
"My name's Joe," said Joe.
"And there are sharks down here, too.
 They especially like to eat pirates."

"Pirates?"
said Simone.

"Pirates!" said Joe.

"COOOOOL!"

said Simone. And Yuto and
Caspar and Mainie and Ibrahim.

And all the kids
seemed happy
with that.

Later, Simone asked, "Do you ever get bored of that question, about your leg, that you don't have?"
"What do *you* think?" said Joe.

Simone *did* know how to answer that.
But Joe had a question of his own.
"Do you still need to know what happened?"

"No!" said
Simone.

And Joe seemed
happy with that.